Looking Back

Looking Back

A Novel by
Daniel Hill Zafren

Published by Time Treasures Books, Goose Creek, South Carolina
www.timetreasuresbooks.com

ISBN: 978-1-7345129-5-3

Cover and interior by Susan Newman Design, Inc.

The earlier memorable books by Daniel Hill Zafren:
In a World We Never Made (2001)
A Door Never Opened (2003)
Shadow Selves (2005)
Network of Death (2006)
Not Lost – Just not Found (2008)
Restless Beauty (2009)
Glimpses of Forgotten Dreams (2010)
Echo in the Heart (2011)
Double Hugs (2011)
Page Passage (2013)
Wish Winds (2014)
Unfinished Thinking (2015)
Vain Regrets (2016)
Network Secret (2016)
Forever Old, Forever New (2017)
Endless Time (2018)
A Gray Voyager (2019)
Right Sight (2020)
Journey to Tomorrow (2020)
A Storm Within (2021)
Unbroken Wings (2022)
The Last Turn in the Road (2023)

LOOKING BACK

We all look back on a life gone by,
Judging it as good or bad is crucial;
The way behind cannot be undone even if we try,
Even if the person is wealthy or unusual.

At the moment it is concluded how it went,
That may be the moment a new trail is set;
For a worthy life is decided how it was spent,
And planning an apt future we want to accept.

One can be harsh or lenient in the hindsight,
The opinions of others can be important;
Accomplishments or failures can be brought to light;
The conclusion can be a revealing moment.

We are who we were and who we now are,
Be it at our grave or at our star!

Daniel Hill Zafren
June 24, 2023

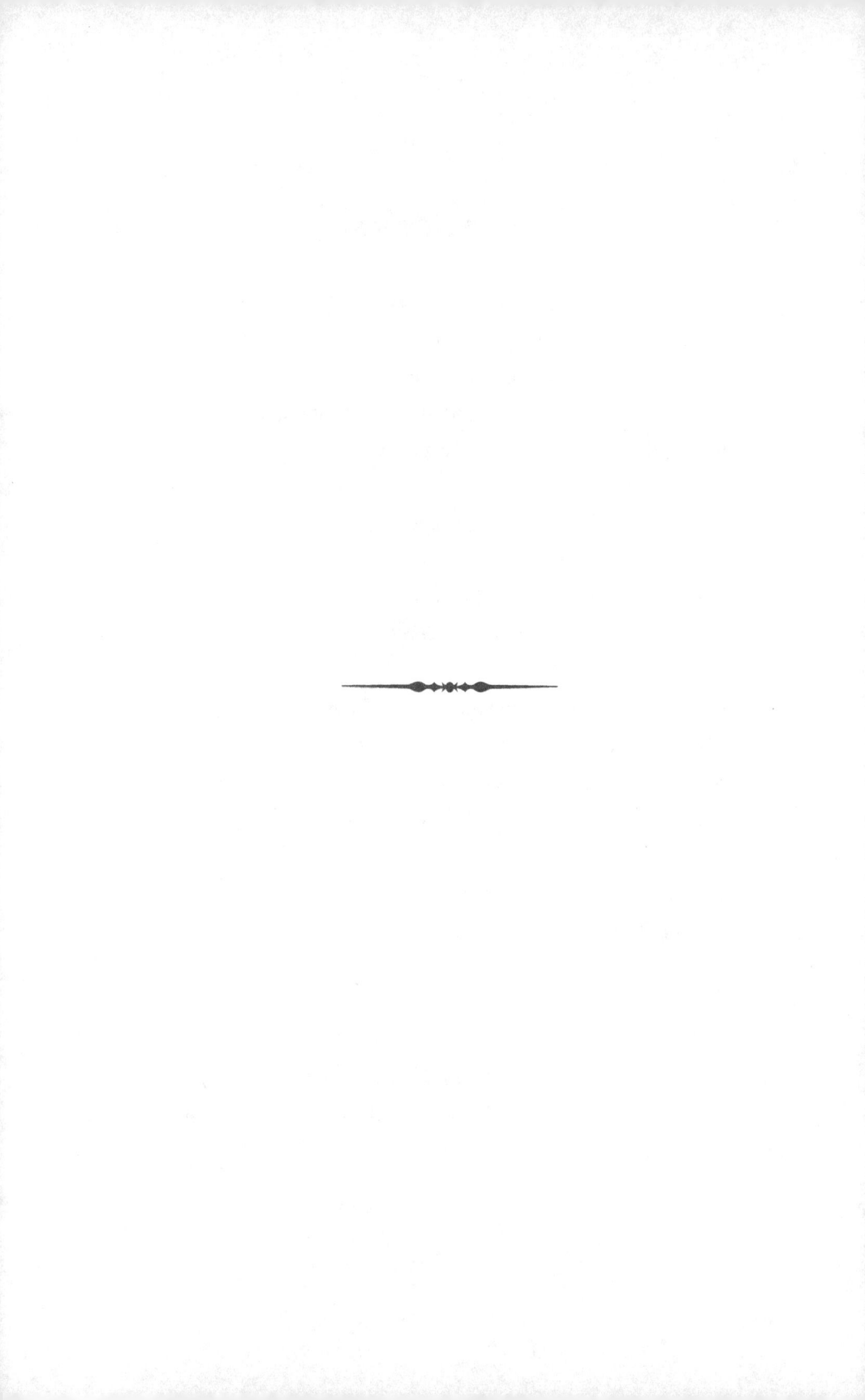

an ending

PROLOGUE

For young people, the large chunk of time lies before them so it is natural for them to look ahead. For old folks, that chunk of time is behind them so they look back. Looking back is not as easy as it sounds. Time has a way of altering events and the perception of them. Memory, or the lack of memory, may even obscure or invent what happened. What should have happened may also lead to a changed set of facts. Talking about it may also be difficult. Yet, the compulsion to look back is powerful and often cannot be denied.

ONE

Would have; could have; should have. If someone asked him to summarize his life, that would be it. Is it polite, or even relevant, to ask an old person to appraise his life? How accurate would that summary be? Would the person be honest about it, forthright, or would failing memory and embarrassment tinge the accounting with more as it might have been than it actually was? And, would anyone really be interested in it anyway? Would anyone want to read a book about it? And, you think young people ask a lot of questions.

He had always had more questions than answers. Maybe, that is why life can be so difficult to fully understand. The answer to one question rarely leads to other answers, but it certainly can lead to many other questions, even a series of questions. Who am I really? Have I done with my life what I was destined to do? Did I get to where I was going on my own? Did I hurt or disappoint others along the way? Were there viable options I never considered? Were there steps that were not taken because of ignorance or fear? Where would I be now if anything had been different?

He no longer recognized the fellow that he saw in the mirror. The image of his former self was completely gone. Perhaps, his former self had wound up in a better place. So, he had to become acquainted with and adjust to the new him, new in the sense of not being confronted before. He would have to deal with it whatever it turned out to be just as he did with everything else. It was as it was and is as it is.

To an outsider, Nathan Holmes had led a good life. He had married his college sweetheart, they had a son and a daughter, and he had become a successful partner in a commercial law firm. Such was certainly the high ground. However, now in old age all of that had lost whatever gloss it may have had. His wife had been deceased now for sixteen years following a debilitating disease, the children were distant and aloof, and a form of forced retirement from the law firm came early after he had lost any motivation to succeed. So, now at the age of eighty-six, he had very little to show as any result of those so-called good years. All seemed to be overtaken by episodes throughout the years of which he was not proud. He had disappointed and hurt others along the way, and his own anguish grew as a form of self-punishment. His inane actions were not intentionally directed to have dire results, but that mattered little as events unfolded. He might rationalize by saying there are little hurts and large hurts, yet a hurt is a hurt and damage can be substantial in either case. Likewise, a series of poor decisions can impact that life so it becomes a mystery rather than a fairy tale.

This was a strange time for him to take stock of his life. There was the one chair in the vacant apartment in which he was sitting. The suitcase was on the floor by his side. He could no longer care for himself, and he was waiting for his son, Albert, to take him to the nursing home for the limited time his doctors said he had left. Neither Albert nor Gwen, his daughter, had offered to take him for the final care. He understood what was going on, and could not really fault their lack of interest in him, and he did not want to be a burden to anyone. Had he nurtured the depths of family earlier, things might be different now. He had put career before family, and that took its toll. It was better this way under the circumstances, although he wished it otherwise. The wishes of a dying old man are carried away in the wind. Piles of such wishes must exist somewhere.

There would be more times ahead in which he would review his life. It might be a futile effort, but it was his rite of crossing over to the future. There was no one better to weigh the good and the bad. His last breath might come before the process was complete, and that itself might mean something.

TWO

Days Ahead was a new specialized nursing home in the area. Because of an array of innovative features, it was partially funded by the State. Albert and Gwen pooled their resources to cover his cost of admission not otherwise funded. Since they had been assured by Nathan's primary physician that his remaining time in this world would be limited, they agreed to do this.

One of the unusual features of the facility was a blend of old and young. The high rise nursing home sat adjoining a child care center. The wall separating the two entities at lobby level was glass so that the elder residents could look out over the playground for the Center and the children could look in to see the older persons in a relaxed lobby setting. It brought a smile to his chapped lips as he was led into the building and saw the children at play. It had been a very long time since he had viewed a scene of such unending wild antics and boundless energy. Any participation he may have had in such a world was far too distant for him to recall.

The potentially short-term residents of the home were assigned rooms on the first floor. Meals were brought in and medical visits scheduled regularly. The rooms were small and sterile, just a single bed, dresser, small table with a lamp, and a lounge chair. Each room had a closet and bathroom. A telephone sat on the table, and a television was mounted on the wall. It would be as good as it gets he decided. A small window looked out over the rear parking lot. In such a setting, he anticipated there would be many opportunities to delve into his past.

Nathan picked at the food on the supper tray sitting on his lap. After it was taken away, he sat in the lounge chair watching the steady rain lash against the window. It was the only sound he heard, and it was soothing to a weary soul. It was a sign of Nature, and he had a deep appreciation of such a natural phenomenon since college days when Hanna had led him to discover what Nature was and could do. As a city raised youngster, he had taken trees, plants, and flowers for granted. She had been raised on a farm, and was able to see beyond the surface to appreciate inner workings and smells. That passion she passed on to him so that he might discover new attributes in old things and appreciate what was new. A road to self-discovery is what she called it. As his love grew for her it was an acknowledgment that she was not like any other woman he had known before. It was also the step forward in the decision that she would be his life partner. She was the perfect blend of simple and complex, and he probably never fully realized the depth of her feelings and capabilities. A mystery woman is how he would describe her, and he never fully appreciated her the way he should have. She always did more for him than he did for her. How he wished she was still here so he could tell her that.

They met during their college freshman year at orientation. She came to the auditorium with her roommate and they sat in the two empty seats besides him. Hanna spoke first, turning to him and speaking in a clear tone, "Have we missed much?"

"Don't think so. Just got here myself." He stared at her profile. There was a small nose slightly tipped up at the end on a finely etched face. Short brown hair had bangs just above the bushy eyebrows above dark brown eyes. The wire-framed glasses seemed perfect for that face. He would not have called her pretty, but since he found himself attracted to her that rarity told him of her allure. Not too many girls had peaked such an interest.

He had not ever been good at conversation, and he wanted to say something witty or profound, but nothing came to mind. She broke the silence, "I bet you thought you would be here alone?"

"I am starting to think that we are never alone."

Her look was intense. "I don't think people are made to be alone."

Before he knew it, he had asked her out on a date. The rest, as they say, is history. A matched pair hooked on each other is not easy to dislodge. They were always together, and he learned that affection can be deep and long-lasting. They counter-balanced one another. He had a tendency to be negative while she tilted on the positive side. He procrastinated and she acted often on impulse. He liked to plan ahead and she lived for the moment. So, things just seemed to work out for mutual benefit.

It did not take him long to discover her love for Nature. On one of their first dates she wanted to go on a picnic in the National Forest adjoining the college campus. She pointed out features of their surroundings that he barely noticed, and whenever they came across scenes or situations that attracted her interest she would supply a commentary to make sure he knew why she was so enthralled.

They married shortly after graduation, and she was able to get a good paying job in the human resources department of a large corporation. She was able to finance all of his law school years and proving how frugal a young married couple can be. Even to this day he admired the sacrifices she made along the way. They lived in a small apartment near the law school. It was not until he landed a job at the law firm and their first child was on the way that they bought a house in the suburbs so she could have the garden she so desired. There would be several houses after that, each larger in size and with corresponding gardens that she created and tended to. She gave extended meaning to a green thumb. There had been no acceptance of the joy of having it all because he did not realize he had it all.

THREE

At a quiet moment, he thought more about his marriage. He had little doubt that she had always been faithful despite the impediments she went along with that could put a strain on any couple. There were long hours worked at the law firm, and it was not uncommon for him to bring work home, and he would be absorbed in that for extended periods of time. There were many business trips, some requiring long absences from the homestead. She was busy tending to the extensive gardens behind the house that she planted and maintained. She made friends easily, and she was close to some of their neighbors. Invitations were plentiful for her presence at many local and social events. If only he could tell her how much he recognized and appreciated all of the sacrifices she made on his behalf.

He had never intentionally planned or wanted to be unfaithful to her. It just seemed to happen and he was not strong enough or principled enough to step away from it. He would usually take the early morning express commuter train to the law firm in the city. He often was on the last train in the evening, home to a late and cold supper with the children off on other pursuits. In the morning, he would read the newspaper or review some office paperwork. On one morning trip, he was dozing when he felt a light tap on his shoulder. When he opened his eyes, he was staring at a young woman. She had long brown hair in a single braid, her complexion clear, and her smile inviting. She handed him a key with a tag attached to it that had an email address and home address on it. She said in a soft voice before she walked away, "This is the key to my back door."

That he was stunned would be an understatement. A red flag rose in his legal mind that he was being targeted for some evil scheme and that he should just ignore it all. Later in the day, after curiosity and perhaps a whim for adventure took hold, he sent a message to the email address on the tag. *While dozing on the train, I had a delightful dream. A mysterious woman handed me a key. An explanation would be helpful.*

Shortly, a response arrived. *I am a lonely single mother who gets on at the same station to go to my advertising job in the city. My mother lives with me and takes care of my daughter. I have studied you for months. You have a kind face and gentle hands. I have finally gotten the courage to take the step to know you.   Lori*

Several communications were exchanged over the following days, and then arrangements made for a meeting. The key fit the back door, and she was waiting just inside wearing a clinging silk dress. It was the start to a relationship that lasted over a year, and together the two found a transport to a rewarding bond that a short life usually denies. The love making was not often, but there was a daily emotional connection and an intellectual discourse that led him to a discovery of the extent of the human mind. He should have felt guilty about what he was doing, but there was a calmness that smothered his senses.   Even today, he was not sure what his true reaction was and should have been. If we always felt uneasy about selfish acts, there would be few quiet moments in life. Why he terminated such pleasure and positive feelings he could not justify, although it just seemed to happen. Her hurt was deep and lasting, and he would never forget the disappointment he saw in her eyes. He had also developed a close relationship with the daughter, Candice, and he was not able to explain to her with any conviction why he was not going to be around anymore. There was a deep hurt there as well, and it lingered all his life to haunt him. Scars in the soul are from wounds that can never fully heal.

Some years later, he was unfaithful again, albeit just one time. He was on a business trip, and it involved meeting with a group of corporate executives. One of them was an especially charming woman, Alice, and after the meeting she suggested she treat him to dinner at the restaurant in his hotel. They went to his room after the meal, and pleasure ruled the night. She left in the morning before he went to the airport, and that was that. Nothing was said as the moment had spoken for itself. Maybe, it was the adventure or the ease of it which taunted his weak character to succumb to a meaningless temptation that further eroded his sensibility and integrity. Without pride in himself, he was less of a husband and father. Philosophically, he could say that the consequences of a delight are worth it, but realistically he knew otherwise. Any moment can be a life long regret.

FOUR

A few days later, after the supper tray was removed Nathan went for a walk down the hall. The door to the room next to his was open. He could not see anyone, and he knocked on the open door. A feeble voice came from the shadows. "I don't want any."

His response was loud, "That's good 'cause I don't have any."

The wheelchair came into view. In it was an old woman, disheveled gray hair obscuring part of a wrinkled face. A thin yellow robe could not hide a small and thin body. She peered at him through large glasses with thick lenses. The voice was even weaker than before. "Whoever you are, I am not buying anything either."

"That's good 'cause anything I might have had to sell has long been gone."

The wheelchair moved closer to him. "Who are you?"

"I have been asking myself that same question."

She stared at him steadily before she spoke. "If you are Dr. Death, I have been waiting for you."

"I am scheduled to see him first, so calm down."

"A stranger can be worse than Dr. Death."

"I am not a stranger either."

"You're a stranger to me."

"I am your neighbor. I am next door."

She did not respond right away. "Be wary of strangers and neighbors."

"Nothing to fear from me. I presume we are waiting for the same thing."

She sneered. "Wanting and waiting are two different things."

"That's a fact."

"You might as well come in and cry on my shoulder as the others do. I look like a witch, sound like one, and they all think I am one. So, I just might as well be. I can only remove curses from the dying."

"You are just the person I need." He walked past her and sat in the lounge chair. He noticed that the bed was still made up, and he figured she probably slept in the wheelchair, either by medical necessity or because there was not enough staff to do such things as help an invalid into the bed.

She pulled the wheelchair close to him and looked at him steadily with eyes that squinted even with glasses on. "You don't look like you are dying."

"I am dead already."

"Nice trick, but you can't fool an old lady or an old witch."

"I don't want to fool an old lady. Fooling myself is enough of a task."

"What is your name?"

"Nat. What is yours?"

"Virginia. It used to be Virgin, but I ain't one so I added the i and the a."

"But still a pistol."

"Better to go out in one shot. Plus, when life has dealt you a bunch of crap, throw it back in their faces."

"I never met a funny witch before."

"You've been missing out much in life, sonny."

"I realize that now more than ever."

"So, how much time do you have left?"

"TBD --- to be determined. And you?"

"They say weeks, but they really mean days."

"Could you use a friend?"

"Can't we all?"

FIVE

Nathan was amazed how quickly a friendship with Virginia was formed, although he probably should not have been since there was so much in common. Being old, infirm, and facing imminent demise, they both looked back on their lives with depressing regret. On the ensuing days, he was in her room more than his own, and the conversation usually ran long and pointed.

She was easy to talk with, and he knew that was why the other floor residents were attracted to her. He did not hold back, and relating the tales of his past was a form of catharsis. He felt good unburdening himself, and he was glad someone else now knew how he felt. As she said, she did not judge anyone as we are all in the final analysis our own judge and jury. Her usual comment was merely to say, "That is a story, alright."

It was also insightful that the first time he had a lengthy talk with her it was not about Hanna, his job, or moments of despair, rather it was about the children. It was understandable how they had become so disenchanted with him. In the formative years, he often was reluctant to spend any time with them. He missed most of the extracurricular activities they may have indulged in. He had considered it a nuisance to attend any of the school plays or athletic events. He dismissed Hanna's plea that he spend more time with them. Discussions were limited, and little advice was asked for or given. Even when they reached adulthood visits were few after Hanna died. He rarely displayed any desire to share in their marriages, the grandchildren, and family occasions. Talking about it perhaps made it worse than it actually was, although Virginia was quick to discern that the guilt matched the crime.

Virginia's story was disjointed, and the gaps in the telling were left to his imagination to fill in. There was a difficult and unrewarding life, no question about that. One of seven children, she had an unfulfilled childhood. She became a teacher and taught for over forty years at the School for the Blind in St. Augustine, Florida. There had been few men interested in her, and she became jaded midst many disappointments. The children she might have had were embodied in the hundreds of students she nurtured at the School. Her annoyance was vented in a warped sense of humor, and she cared little who she cast aside or belittled. "I came to the conclusion that you can tell when a person is lying by when their lips move."

The Fountain of Youth is located in St. Augustine. Virginia made a point of drinking from it regularly, but there were no desired results. She grew older, became the object of varying illnesses, and had to give up teaching. She lived with one of her sisters until home care became difficult and the nursing home solution the only option. She wallowed in the remnants of an empty life. What keeps her going at this point is the companionship of the other first floor residents who feel at ease in her company and who relate tales of lives lived, lives dreamed about, and lives stolen. Even though she had finally received what might be considered full training to become a witch, there is really little calling for such a pursuit. If she would have known then what she knows now, she would have become a witch at an early age and made sure that she could mess up as many lives as she could. That way she might have salvaged a place for herself.

SIX

Through Virginia Nathan quickly became acquainted with the other first floor residents. It is true that old folks like to talk about their ailments. A close second in the discussion field, however, is a discourse on how they messed up their lives and what they should have done differently. As Nathan could attest to, there really are no viable second chances. Beating oneself up about it does not do any good. Yet, misgivings can linger. They probably should linger as the price one paid for a mistake, made by accident or intentionally. Often, wisdom comes too late.

He listened intently to all the tales of woe, and while he dared not offer any advice he did try to soothe agitation with an encouraging or sympathetic word. He found himself less likely to talk about his own past now, not wanting his own miseries to add to anybody's burden. He was discovering that in his own aging process, such were becoming more private. There was also the stark recognition that since he could not undo the past he might just as well live with it until he was gone. A memory ends when life ends.

Florence Chadwick was the most talked about first floor resident. Besides appearing in an assortment of minor roles in Broadway shows, she boasted to all that she had been married five times. Stories about the attributes and antics of the first four husbands might make you shake your head in disbelief that such behavior might exist. There were beatings, infidelity, criminal activity, and a host of disagreeable attitudes and behavior. Even the five children that she bore during that period were either physically or mentally impaired. Finally, the fifth husband turned out to be the ideal companion, but he died eighteen months after the wedding. Just the mention of his existence or even just saying his name and the tears would flow. She had finally gotten it right, and then it was all taken away from her. She warmly hugged Nathan when he offered his shoulder to cry on.

There were just two other male residents on the first floor. Arnold Gold, age eighty-one, a body riddled with cancer, did not move or talk much. He was bed-ridden, and Nathan only heard about him through the others. Evidently, his life had been difficult although few knew the details.

John Jenkowski, age seventy-four, was a short and stocky man who was quiet and withdrawn. He had not confided his story to Virginia. He was considered a man of mystery. One day, when Nathan had the door to his room open, he looked up and saw John coming in with his walker. "Mind if I park myself for awhile?," he asked in a meek voice.

"No, by all means. Find a comfortable spot and stay as long as you like."

The walker had its own seat, so John moved to the window and sat there. He gazed out the window to a world which he knew he would never be a part of him again. "You have made friends quickly. Virginia tells me you have a sympathetic ear."

"I like to think so. I am no problem solver, as measured by my own life, but to be able to listen is a large part of understanding."

"I have little time left. I want someone to know my story. I have no family, and the few friends I had are either dead or now distant."

"Old age is a time to close the doors."

"When I look back on my life, I see one big regret. It haunts me."

"I know it is of little actual comfort, but you are not alone."

"People might conclude I have had a satisfying life. On the surface that might be true. I was a specialist with the Veteran's Administration and worked with the blind at VA hospitals all around the country. The downside was that I was moved all around the country, never being in one place for more than a year or two. There was little time for building relationships or finding friends. One day, when I was fifty seven, I had a revelation. There had been only one woman in my life that I truly loved, and she was a woman who loved me as no other had or probably could. It was my college sweetheart. I had killed that relationship because I failed to fully realize what I had, and I had an immature desire to roam and be free. How foolish in hindsight. So, I decided to try and reconnect with her. To try and make up for my mistake. As a shock that tears me apart, I discovered that she had died two years earlier after a long illness, leaving behind a husband, a daughter, and three grandchildren. I was devastated. I should have been the one with her all along, especially through her final days. I was never the same after that. Even the satisfaction of helping the veterans did nothing for me. I retired as soon as I was able to and became a hermit until my own body started to punish me. I await to join my love in the after world."

Nathan did not know what to say. Words cannot soothe all feelings, and they certainly cannot attempt to justify what one has decided was a tragic fault. "I, too, live with regrets about things I did or didn't do. There may not be any greater pain."

"Death is the great equalizer."

"Can I do anything for you?"

"Nothing can be done. Absolutely nothing. Thanks for listening. It helps just knowing that someone else knows." With that, he left.

Nathan stood at the doorway for awhile, noting that looking back for all of us is and can be many different things. The futility of it all is what sears the soul.

SEVEN

Nathan did not sleep well that night. In fact, sleeping had become difficult most of the time, and even when he did sleep it was fitful. This time he had an added obstacle to the rest his body and mind coveted. John's story was relived over and over again except now he was the main character. Hanna had been his college sweetheart, and although he did not let her go and did marry her his devotion to her was less than exemplary. He had not done for her all that he might have, and he was not the kind of partner that she deserved. He had loved her, but was that enough? He was grateful for the sacrifices she made for him, not to mention the daily actions that fortified his being. Besides his unfaithful actions, had he been there for her when she needed support? It further made him analyze himself in terms of his humanity. He should have been kinder and more giving. He certainly should have been more understanding.

It was evident that his guilt was leading to a form of self-punishment. Yet, his character was the culprit. He knew many people wished that they could relive their lives. He earnestly desired that to atone for the many misgivings he had. As he faced death he wanted to become a better person. Was it too late for that? Would there be any solace in the final days? Two ideas came to mind. He could attempt to alleviate some of the doubts and regrets of the other first floor residents, and he might attempt to reach out to his son and daughter so that their last memory of him might salvage some of the earlier failures. He might not be able to change who he had been, but he might be able to change who he is. A daunting task under the best of circumstances.

Just thinking about Hanna and the memories flooded in. The first kiss on the first date. They had gone to a movie, and during the show she was the one that moved her hand to grasp his. Her fingers were warm and soft, and he felt that it was a perfect fit. They went to an ice cream parlor and shared a huge sundae. She wiped a blob of whipped cream from his lips and placed it against her own lips. They shared the feeling of being away from home and experiencing a new kind of loneliness. As they approached her dormitory, she pulled him into the shadow of a large bush. He bent down to kiss her waiting lips and it was as if it sealed a pact.

The first time they made love was etched in his mind as if in stone. He had not been experienced with women and he was not really sure what to do in a way that would satisfy her. It mattered not as she led him through their ecstasy. It was her first time as well, and since they had been picnicking in a remote spot in the woods, that fact led a gloss for her because it was outdoors and was in line with her love of Nature. It was also the first time she openly declared her love for him. He had expressed that sentiment numerous times along the way.

In the early years, in the marital bed she would sleep in his arms. As time passed, that closeness seemed to evaporate without them being fully aware of it. That was too bad now that he looked back on it. If he had made a conscious effort to maintain bodily closeness, he might have been better at keeping an all around closeness. If he had done even a small fraction of the things that he had thought about doing, perhaps he would have eased her path and made her eventual death easier to accept.

When one is facing death, since there is no window to the future, the window to the past becomes a major part of life. That window may not be clear to see through, and with added failing eyesight what is seen may actually not be a true representation of what had been. But, that is what must be dealt with. Looking back through that window at things undone and at words unsaid, there can be much pain. Some of the good moments might ease the pain at times, and may even bring a smile to chapped lips. Emotions can be mixed, and complications can arise in keeping places and events in proper order. Yet, looking back may be all that there is.

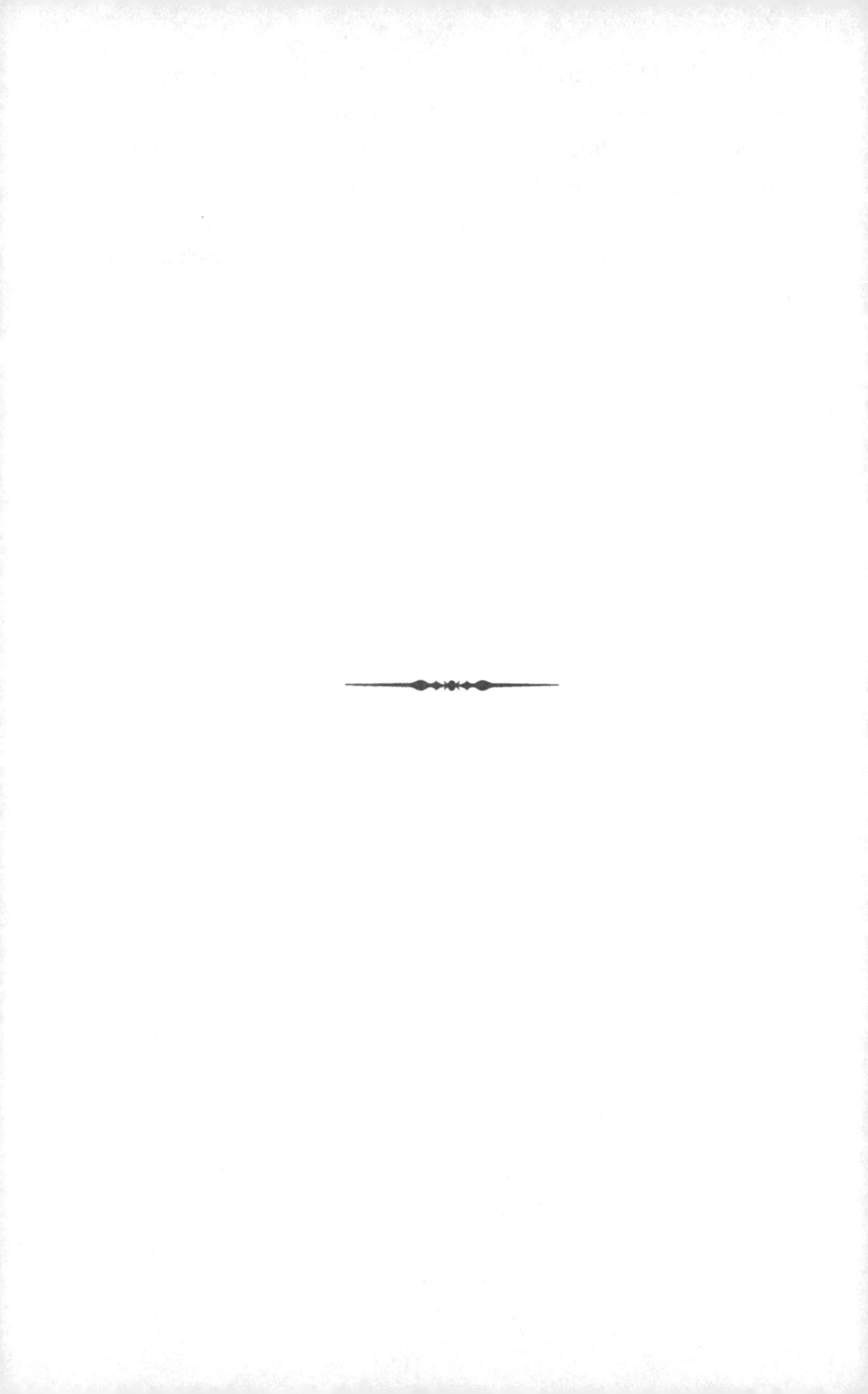

EIGHT

An eerie silence fell over the first floor. Two deaths on the same day was an unspoken message and a sinister omen. Arnold Gold died in his sleep. Virginia Calloway died in the afternoon, a shriek piercing the hallway as a dramatic announcement of a life expired.

Now that Virginia was gone, the remaining residents, as well as the two new ones that quickly filled the vacancies, gravitated to Nathan to unburden themselves as if he had been Virginia's hand-picked successor. He tried to be as encouraging as possible. When encouragement was not enough, he used his long abandoned attorney diplomacy. He also employed Virginia's concept of Dr. Death coming as a way to describe the impending end. This adopted role suited him, and he felt good about what he was doing. This was reflected in his own physical condition. He had not felt this robust in quite some time.

He debated with himself whether he should invite both Albert and Gwen in at the same time, or meet with them separately. He decided it would be best if they came at the same time. He would be spared repeating himself, and it might be helpful if they could interact with each other.

Upon receipt of their father's request, Albert and Gwen talked it out between them. Their initial reaction was to just ignore the invitation to meet with them as he had ignored them throughout their lives. Any emotional upheaval would be avoided. It would probably just be a dying man's attempt at garnering pity. After thrashing it out, they decided to meet with him. It would be a form of closure to say goodbye.

Days Ahead had set aside several private decorated lounges off of the lobby for residents to meet with visitors since the rooms were too small for such events. Nathan went to the one he reserved early so that he could fully prepare himself and be assured that he would not miss them in case they arrived early.

There was no hand shaking or embracing. Albert and Gwen merely nodded to him and sat in the two armchairs across from him that he pointed to.

"Thank you both for coming," Nathan began in as strong a voice as he could muster. "I am sure your heart is not totally in it, but I have newly discovered that the request of a dying person is a force to be reckoned with. A dying man spends much time looking back, and I believe that because of my actions, or I should say lack of actions, I have been dead long ago as far as you see it and feel it. If I could take it all back, I would. Painfully, I fully realize that I was not the kind of father you both deserved, as well not the kind of husband your mother deserved. She was a wonderful woman, and every facet of her being as I look back on it confirms that fact over and over again. I may have wanted to be all of the husband that she needed and wanted me to be, but I wasn't. As I look back, I wasted those precious years too as far you are involved. I did not share in your growing emotionally and mentally. I did not give you the love and support that a youngster needs to confront the world and fit into the throng. I have not even shared in your adult lives and your families. I did not even redeem myself with a second chance by participating in the growth of my grandchildren. I might have been a role model, but flubbed that chance as well. I realize we all lost much in our family history. I can see that your pain was spread out over the years. Mine has been dumped on me all at once."

Nathan hesitated for a moment seeing a tear from at the corner of Gwen's eye. For the first time he realized how much she looked like

Hanna, and it was another cruel reminder of his messed up past. "I am truly sorry for all of this. There is no excuse for it, and there is no way to justify it. I am just hoping that you can take some solace in my expressions of guilt and can, even after I am long gone, forgive me. In my closing days I am trying to be a better person, the kind of person I should have been all along. And, while it might ring hollow, I do love you both. Unfortunately, I never let that love do any good for any of us. Thank you again for coming here today and thank you for listening. I can face my final days better knowing that I expressed my thoughts."

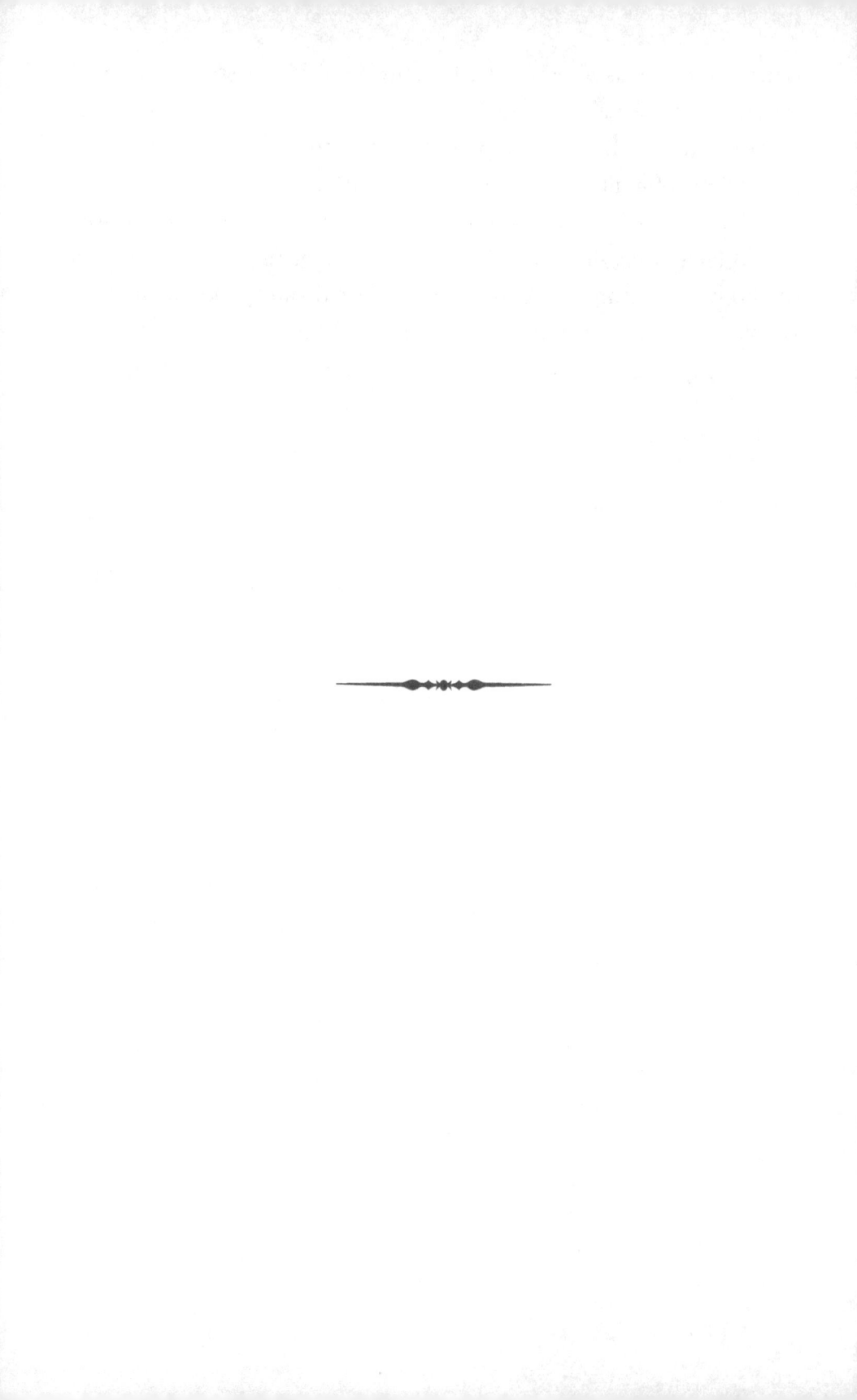

NINE

There was probably no way Nathan would ever know whether his overture to the children was the right thing to have done, but he felt it was so and that was probably all that mattered at this point. He hoped that they had taken some comfort away from it as well.

The meeting with Gwen and Albert left him with a rash of memories about Hanna. Talking about her was almost like being with her again, and the memories emerged. He could not sleep that night. He sat in the chair in the dark staring out the window into the blackness. In his first year at the law firm, Hanna asked him to plan his vacation for the Fall because she wanted to drive through New England to see the changing color of the leaves. She had always had a fascination with this phenomena. She had planned a thousand mile trip, mainly through the scenic byways, and with stops each night at a Bed and Breakfast inn. On the drive, she would gush with delight if they came across a particularly striking splash of color. Her enthusiasm would carry over to the nightly stops and she would pour forth intricate descriptions of their escapade to the proprietors of the inns. Each breakfast was unique and very satisfying, and he could almost taste them anew in his mind.

The first Christmas after they were married, Hanna wanted to do something to help others. That had been a driving force for her throughout her lifetime. Giving was always better than getting she would say. So, they volunteered at the local food shelter to be on the soup line for the homeless on that Christmas day. He saw it as clearly as he did on that day as he admired her mannerism. As the homeless filed by and they filled their plates with hot items to partake of, with each person she would flash her warm smile and she would say something personal and uplifting. It would bring a smile or an utterance of appreciation from the homeless person, and that was an additional reward for an exceptional woman. A remarkable feature of Hanna that alone should have endeared her to him for a lifetime was that it took very little to satisfy her or to make her happy.

In Hanna's final days, Nathan described that venture to her in an attempt to lift her spirits. She was unable to remember it, the pain obliterating much of any focus on the past. A solitary memory for a loving couple is a sad moment in life's end.

Remembering events and people can often be difficult for any person, and a shared memory can present additional difficulties. Even impressions that linger can change in many ways.

As the residents of the first floor took him in their confidence, much of their outpourings were memories. They were branches of life's tree that they might cling to break a fall to the ground. They would try to justify the memory itself as long as they had the ability to remember something. A young person uses experiences to build up their composite picture. An old person uses memories to hold that composite picture together. In either case it may be crucial to do it.

There were many memories for Nathan, a man who was often confused about his role in life. It was ironic that clarity came in the final days, a clarity which might help others but not himself. He would have to accept that as there was little choice when death was close. As much as he might wish it otherwise, that was the way it was. He just needed to be stoic about it.

TEN

By this time, a man in Nathan's position should have everything in his life in order. If he considered the meeting with Albert and Gwen a matter to have been taken care of, perhaps he could say that all was in order. There was nothing else to consider. He had no assets, no property, and no personal items of any value or significance. That, too, was a sad commentary on a man's life.

He was not alone among the first floor residents to ponder the lack of a life before it was nearly over, especially the reasons for such a sad state of being. Likewise, most of them were haunted by the ghosts of the past. All he could really do was to listen to the anguish, as he could offer little comfort or advice. Yet, he felt just the listening was a form of help. A hug and a shoulder to cry on was of some solace.

Annette Winslow visited him on several occasions, anxious to bare her soul, repeating the two ghastly instances of her past which tormented her and fashioned a life in decline after such occurrences. Events can shape or misshape a future. Her body trembled throughout the telling. In her early thirties, she was driving down a lonely street early before dawn. Before she knew it directly in front of the car headlights a large dog emerged. The lights caught the instant terror in the dog's eyes, and the resulting thud of a dead body hitting the pavement resonated in her ears. It was an experience that jolted her well being. It was not even two months later that she was driving down a busy street in broad daylight when a young boy darted out into the street from between two parked cars chasing after a ball. For an instant she saw the terror in his eyes as he looked in her direction, and she heard the same kind of thud of a dead body falling to the street. After that, there was no quiet life, no peace. Her guilt obliterated any chance of normalcy, no opportunity to redeem the two deaths she caused.

Gloria Beslow told a heart-wrenching story of her past that defined her ongoing depression. She had done everything possible a mother could do for her daughter, Trudy. She had done even beyond the usual actions. This included taking care of her for an entire year when she was in a fullbody cast. That involved caring for her every need as well as turning her numerous times during the day. There was never any gratitude expressed for such a devotion. In fact, she was rather vindictive and caused unnecessary problems for Gloria along the way. It is truly sad when a child turns on a parent for no reason.

There is a popular misconception that older people do not have the same kind of feelings as young people have. Not true at all. Their feelings are the same, maybe even more accentuated depending on the circumstances. The only difference may be that seniors understand those feelings better, and as such can mask them if the consequences demand it.

Added to the issues that the other residents heaped on him, Nathan had to face a staggering reality. The latest visit by the doctor was disheartening. After finding out that the current medications he was on were ineffective and were failing to help him cope with the pain, a new medicine was prescribed with the caveat that it too may prove to be helpless. It was, however, something Nathan surmised that was designed to hasten his demise rather than prolong his existence. He thought about not taking the medicine at all, but then reconsidered that and since everyone else wanted him dead he might as well join the consensus.

ELEVEN

Memory loss is a dynamic topic among the elderly. Young people have little, if any, understanding or sympathy about such a plight. All of the first floor residents have expounded to Nathan about some anxiety and even fear about memory loss. Nathan tried to categorize such occurrences as annoying and frustrating while avoiding dreaded results. He defined memory loss in three basic groups: not completely remembering an event or person in the past; remembering an occurrence in the past, but not accurately about any of the facts about it, such as place, time, or participants; and remembering an event of the past which really never happened. Some of the residents experienced only one category, while others intertwined among all of them. His own memory loss probably crossed all of the lines and then some.

He attempted to give some hope to a resident when a tale was extremely draining. Hope, too, could, as he calculated it, come in many shapes and sizes. He bolstered an ego or downtrodden thoughts by painting some bright side not thought of before. If all else failed, he could at least give the person something else to think about. He would say something like, "When you are still alive, there has to be a reason for it."

By helping these folks, Nathan believed in some form it might make up for instances when he could have helped others and he did not. It most instances it would have taken little effort and yet might have made a huge difference for the person seeking aid. These kind of small tragedies, as he referred them to, were as tiny daggers to his being.

His actions and reactions with the first floor residents soon became a matter of interest and discussion with other residents of the home as well as the staff. Folks from other floors would come to the first floor to see this man who apparently held the secret to many of life's problems. Issues among the elderly stretch far beyond the possibility of imminent death. Some would engage him in conversations about a multiple of problems of aging testing his so-called mountaintop wisdom. They would return to their respective floors to ponder what he might have said or even left unsaid when alluded to. Nathan came to think of it as a game. Let them fill in the blanks he would say to himself.

His reputation reached even beyond the home. Residents would tell their visitors about the reputation he had garnered. Visitors would tell others, and soon a reporter for the local newspaper got wind of it and came to interview him. That led to an engrossing story in the paper. Nathan mailed copies of the article to Albert and Gwen. They needed to know that in the end, as the story revealed, many thought he was a guru.

TWELVE

Nathan wondered if and when he might know his death was close. The answer came more clearly than he thought it would. As he sat in the chair staring out in the blackness of the night, a strange yet comforting feeling filtered through his body. It defied description and yet demanded acceptance. All of his pain was gone, even though he had stopped taking his medication. There was a great lucidity to his thoughts and to forgotten memories that came to him. The crevices of his life experiences seemed to fill themselves in. These sensations stayed with him as he prepared himself for bed.

He lay in the bed, the darkness hovering over him. In the darkness a bright and colorful image of Hanna appeared, and it was inviting him to reach out and clutch it. Without a doubt she had been the most vital part of his life, and it was reasonable that she should be here in the closing moments. Never really acknowledging it at any point, his love for her was the essence of his existence, and he was now taking that essence in his death. He lovingly embraced that image as he closed his eyes for the last time.

For a man who failed in so many ways, he finally did leave behind the accomplishment of trying to help others to ease their final moments or find the hidden meaning of times gone by. For a man who really had nothing and who in life did little to be proud of, he did leave behind a legacy after all.

a beginning

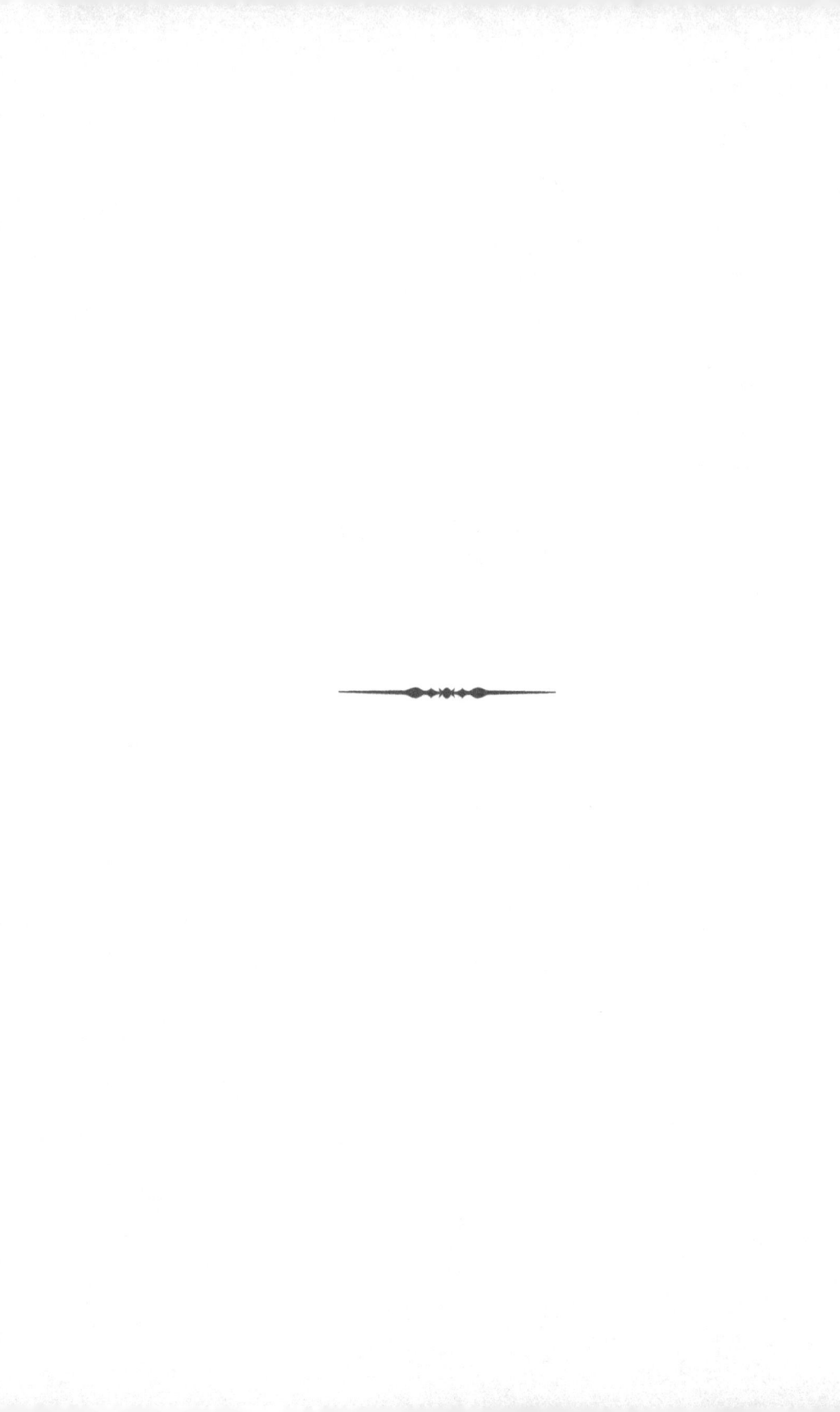

PROLOGUE

Life is strange. Death can be even stranger. One can rightfully conclude that death ends a life. Yet, such may not be the actual effect. While living, a person's influence on others may be greater only after being gone. One only can look to the great writers, poets, artists, and composers, to realize that an influence long beyond death can be extensive. For the ordinary person, the example may not be quite so clear, but nevertheless it may be as effective. A memory of that person, in whole or in part, may inspire an action that would not have happened otherwise. That memory can also alter an outlook or prompt a dream. A memory of one gone may affect a living being in many ways. In fact, for some it may be so pervasive that for all intents and purposes the one gone may seem to still be here.

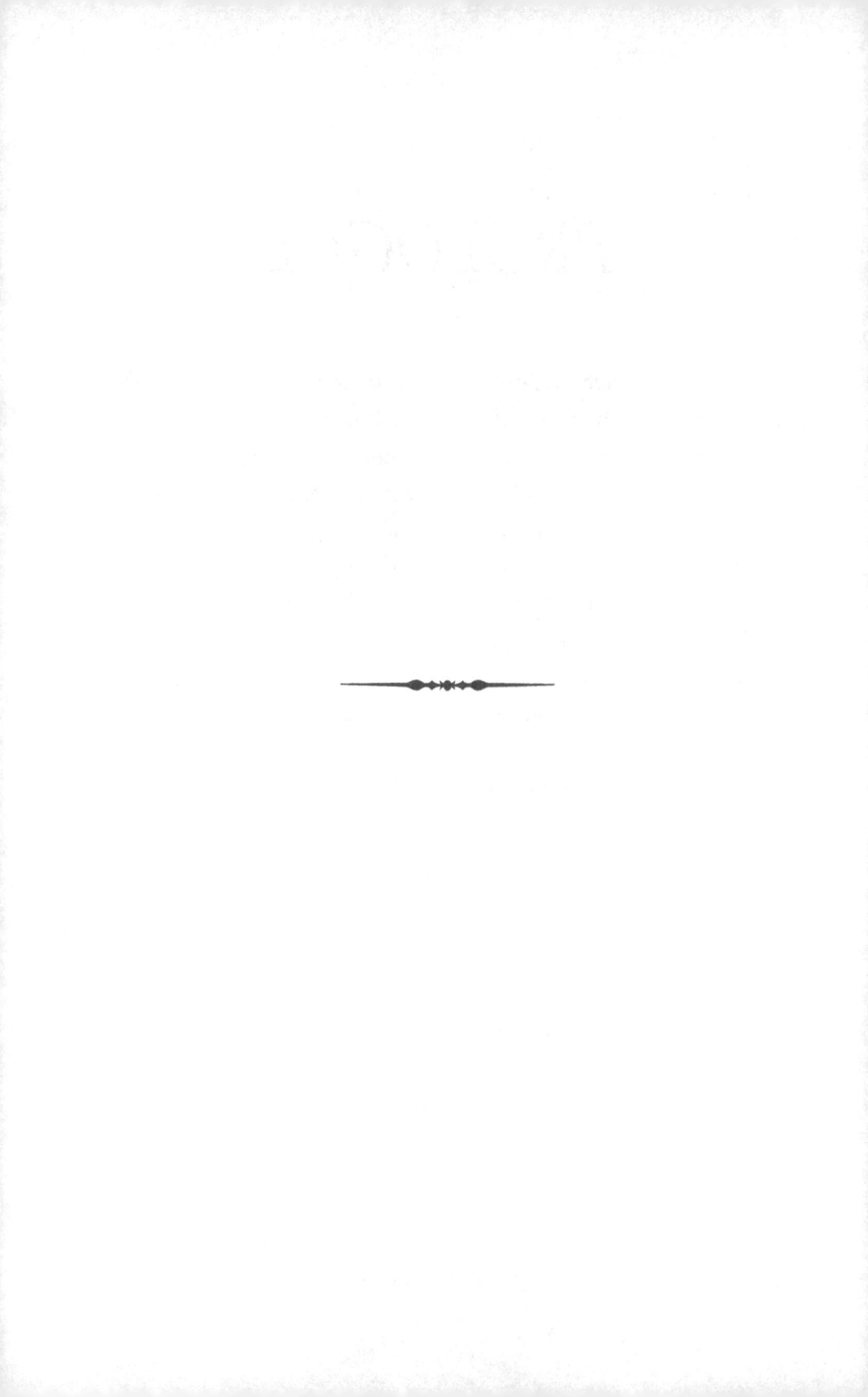

A

Gwen stared at the newspaper article on her desk. It was about a man doing wonderful things for those facing death in a nursing home, a man who was her father, a man she really never knew. Yet, there was an underlying connection that she knew was there. So, when Albert called to tell her that Nathan had passed, she cried over a stranger's demise.

Albert had always been close to her even though they were so different. Their mother had always nurtured that relationship. Albert was highly disciplined and matter-of-fact about everything. If there was no logical reason for an action, he would dismiss it. He rarely displayed his emotions, and he was careful about making decisions and slow to plan ahead. He was a strict and attentive father to his three children, and devoted to his wife, Serena. Gwen was much more sensitive. She was more at ease with people and in situations, and actions and decisions came quickly, at times too quickly. At their mother's funeral and burial, Gwen sobbed uncontrollably while Albert was stone-faced. If he was distraught he would not want anybody to see it.

Nathan was buried in the plat next to Hanna's grave. They had purchased those adjoining plats early on when at the law firm Nathan had handled a matter for the cemetery and in appreciation for his service they gave him a greatly reduced price for the burial places. At the time, Nathan thought he would later resell them, but he never did.

Gwen was the only one at the burial. Albert refused to be there, and he was content to know that a chapter in their lives was finally over.

Gwen did not think she would cry, although she did. The tears were genuine and they flowed freely. Tears flowing was renewed when she kissed her mother's grave stone. Nathan had been distant to her. Yet, in that final meeting and rereading the newspaper article several times, her thoughts about Nathan had changed. She not only thought she would have liked to have known him better, she also felt that perhaps he was, after all, the kind of person she would have liked to have had as a father. He was then more of a father in death than he had been in life. His influence on her feelings and thoughts would bring about big changes for her in her life.

B

The impact of Nathan's death stayed with Gwen over the following days. It led her to examine her own life, an action she had refrained from doing before. She was nothing except a middle-aged suburban housewife who really did nothing and had almost nothing to boast about or hold on to. She had married Karl soon after graduating from college. They had met at a wedding, and the novelty of him wanting to be with her swept her up in romantic dreams. He had a good job as a stock analyst, and he gave her expensive gifts and took her to fancy restaurants. She was not sure that she loved him, but Albert encouraged the union seeing that she would want for nothing in a comfortable marriage. She now fully realized after being frank with herself, even after more than thirty years, that a comfortable marriage was the last thing that she needed and wanted.

The one positive she could dwell on, and often obscured the total picture, was with Casey, their daughter. Now eighteen, Casey was about to go off to Cornell University, and for all intents and purposes, beyond her daily care and participation in her life. Because Hanna was such a wonderful mother, and who went above and beyond to compensate for Nathan's parental failures, Gwen had been a good mother to Casey. They were very close, and she was proud about the kind of person Casey had become. She was a caring and vibrant individual capable of doing anything she set her mind out to do.

She thought long and hard about the marriage to Karl. Basically, he was a good man, although he was not fully attentive to her needs and wants. It seemed that his main concern was that dinner was ready when he returned home from work. Any conversations between them were short and without substance. Besides Casey, there was little they shared in common. Besides an occasional meal at a restaurant, they did little together. He was absorbed in sports, and would be glued to the television many a night. She had made friends in the neighborhood, but he showed little interest in their husbands or doing anything socially with any of them. Any love making was brief and infrequent, and she was left unsatisfied. Even as she grew older, she desired a fulfilling male contact. Life was too short not to go after a dream. Nathan's life proved that it was never too late to do what one should do to pursue happiness and personal fulfillment.

She did not discuss her thoughts and feelings with Albert, and what she was about to do. He would not approve of it and would try to talk her out of it. She would tell him about it afterwards. His disapproval would then be just a matter of history.

C

Just the right opportunity arose that Friday night. Casey had gone to a friend's house for a sleep over, so Gwen and Karl were alone. After dinner, they went to the den to watch television.

"Before you turn the television on," she began in a low tone, "I would like to have a talk with you."

He sat in the arm chair across from her. "Fire away."

"I don't know if you have been aware of it or not, but I have been unhappy for a long time. I did not know why until recently. I can't explain why, but the recent death of my father has served as a form of catalyst for me to put my mind and heart together to help me understand myself. The life we live is not the kind of life I want to live." She could see that he was getting fidgety. "This is all me. I am not at ease or content living in the suburbs and going through the daily motions that thousand of others do. While my mother had her gardens, I am not at all interested in flowers or plants. The house is just a place to sleep. There is little contentment being in it or caring for it. I must have been in some kind of trance all this time to have tolerated it."

Karl interrupted her, his defense mode kicking in. "I felt something was wrong, but I did not think you were that unhappy. I do not know how to approach you. We have a comfortable life here. There are thousands of people who would gladly trade places with us."

She could tell that this was not going to go well with him, so she better not even bring up that he is not the kind of husband she wanted.

"I am not thousands of others, and it does not mean that I can't want something else."

He threw up his hands in a small display of disgust, his voice raised accordingly. "I just don't understand you, Gwen. Casey will be gone soon, and it will be just the two of us. We can do things we might not have considered before, such as taking a long trip somewhere if you want to get away for awhile."

It was obvious he did not understand her. He would further not understand what she was about to say. "I want to live in the city. I want to be part of city life, and to take advantage of all the cultural and other events it has to offer. I want to live in an apartment where I have nothing to worry about taking care of a place."

He lashed out, "And how do you plan to manage that?"

"You stay here and keep the house. I will have to dip into our joint funds to get started, but I plan to be self-sufficient. I will get a job. I majored in Sociology, and should be qualified to become a social worker."

"I suppose I should have known you are a dreamer. If this is what you think you want to do, go do it, but there will be no turning back. Once you leave, there will be no crawling here."

"I fully realize that everything in life has consequences."

"What am I going to say to Casey?"

"That is my problem. Please know that I do not blame you for anything. You are a good man and have always been good to me. I will always appreciate that."

"Following a dream, and a cock-eyed one at that, does not mean you are going to wind up anywhere. I have known people with lofty ideas who have started out strong only to wind up at a dead end."

"If so, I will have no one to blame but myself. Now, I don't look back. I look ahead."

D

Gwen knew that telling Casey what was going on would be easier, and it was. It would be confrontational with Albert, but that would be the last hurdle.

On Saturday, Gwen and Casey were alone in the house. It would take something such as a hurricane or tornado for Karl to miss his usual Saturday golf game. That his wife was leaving him was certainly not a strong enough reason to skip the golf game.

Casey guessed something was going on when Gwen suggested they sit in the kitchen alcove. If she had to guess, it would be another lecture on her forthcoming venture to Cornell. However, it was not a complete surprise when it was about the collapse of the marriage. She was astute enough to know that there was an empty marriage, and she often picked up on her mother's behavior and attitude that things were wrong. That her mother wanted to break free and pursue a life on her own was a surprise, but it was one that she could relate to. Casey visualized for herself a life that she could control and be happy with.

"So, that is it, Casey," Gwen said conclusively.

Casey hugged her. "It's much to take in, but I am not shocked. Your marriage is not one I would wish for myself, so I can understand you wanting to break away from it. It may all prove for you that there is still a life out there you want and I wish that you find it and enjoy it."

"I knew that you, of all people, would understand. It is going to be more of a battle with your uncle Albert than it was with your father."

"That will be his problem," Casey said sternly.

"I am not so sure about that."

Talking to Albert alone was also a problem, but she managed to schedule some time that even he could not dodge. After describing her plans in as glowing terms as possibles, Albert stormed around the room, his voice so elevated that one standing beyond the house could have heard him clearly. "I thought I knew you, Gwen, but it is evident I didn't. I don't understand any of this. You have an ideal and secure life. Why would you give that up? What do you really think lies out there for you? I can tell you that you are headed for great disappointment, and Karl will not take you back. Neither will I. Our father was a dreamer. I thought that you realized that and that dreams are for the foolish. You saw how he wound up. Do you want that for yourself? And, what kind of role model are you presenting now for Casey? Do you want her to wander through life or to actually set on goals that are worth achieving? I thought I would not have to worry about you in the years ahead. I can see that my worrying is just getting started. Think about it. There is still time to make this right by giving up this nonsense. Do you really think that this will make you a strong woman? You are already strong because you have a worthy life, a life where you can have whatever you need. Don't give that up? Reconsider this absurd idea."

The best way to diffuse another person's argument is by ignoring it. Where or when Gwen had read that she could not recall. "Albert, you can rant and rave all you want to, but this is my life and this is going to be the way that it is."

E

Until recent events, Gwen had never thought of her life in terms of fate. Now, it seemed as if she was putting all of her faith in that concept. Each step would be new, and each step would have to be bold. Perhaps, she had wasted enough time on a form of life she was now abandoning. A revelation for a person of any age.

Was it fate or just a stroke of good luck that she found an apartment right away not only in the center of the metropolis, but it also had an expansive view of the river as well as coming with an underground parking space for her car? Broad horizons centered around personal comfort. Whatever and whenever she would value and appreciate advances.

To at least partially furnish the new abode, the contents of the guest room from the house were moved to the new place. Since Karl was not being cooperative, and would not even speak with her, she did not seek his permission. No sense traveling down a dead end road.

Gwen had dearly loved her mother, and throughout her life her mother was her role model. After she was gone, whenever a decision loomed ahead Gwen would speculate on what her mother would do in that kind of situation. Now, there was a new factor that entered into that equation. She would wonder what her father would say or do. She was sure that Albert would think that was strange, but it made a deep and lasting impression on her. Was his ending her beginning?

No time was wasted in looking for a job. The ideal would be

a day job during the week leaving the nights and weekends free to pursue the cultural activities available. Since the municipal building was around the corner from the apartment, she started the search there. A job with the City would have certain additional advantages such as a retirement plan and heath insurance.

That turned out to be a stroke of good fortune or a tickle of fate, as the City had just posted openings for newly created positions of wellness counselors. People with cars were needed to visit the two hospitals and six nursing homes within the City limits to check on patients and residents to assure that quality standards were being met. Her sociology education seemed an appropriate fit.

Within three weeks she was interviewed and approved to fill one of these positions. She would cover four of the nursing homes. Gwen was pleased and excited about the prospects. The newspaper article about Nathan and his accomplishments at the nursing home flashed before her eyes. No doubt there was a connection here with her father, and she wondered if the fate she was relying on was also going to carry her on to do what he had pursued.

The future she was about to meet would answer all of her questions and allay any of her doubts. She was eager to move on. Gwen sent a nightly text to Casey keeping her informed. On the news of the job, Casey's response was emphatic, "Go for it, mom!"

F

After a week of training, Gwen was ready to go out in the field. Given a computer for her reports, the template for each report showed all of the pertinent data that she could just fill in the blanks with ample room for comments and suggestions.

The Sunset Nursing Home was four blocks from her apartment, and she thought that she would start there. It was close enough to walk to, but she drove there just in case she had to go somewhere else after that. It was the first day on the job and she was not sure what to expect although prepared for anything.

The Director of the Home, Maggie Fletcher, gave her a tour of the facility. She suggested that Gwen talk with Florence Ecsatz, the longest resident at the home. Florence, at age 97, had been there for thirteen years and no longer had any visitors since all of her relatives and friends had passed away.

Florence was in a wheelchair in the sunroom at the back of the building. Gwen pulled up a chair and sat next to her after introductions were concluded. "I am a Counselor with the City and would like to talk with you for awhile if you don't mind."

Gwen noted how frail Florence seemed to be, and she was not sure that she heard her. The voice was not as weak as Gwen would have guessed. "Don't get visitors and don't talk much, but at my age I don't need much of an incentive to do anything."

"You seem to be doing alright."

"Doing and being are two different things. You are young. Your time will come."

"My father recently passed at a home. He clued me in to some of the things I should prepare myself for."

Florence smirked. "You can't prepare yourself. Growing old is the crossroads and directions are far from clear. Children are guided to adulthood, but it stops there. You can try to make adulthood what you think you want it to be. Old age controls you and makes you what it wants you to be."

Gwen was impressed by the thinking and expressions of the oldster. "Are you well taken care of here?"

Florence ignored the question. "No matter who you are or who you are with, old age is a lonely place."

"One can be lonely at any age."

"Ah, but there are different kinds of loneliness. I am talking about emptiness with no chance of fulfillment."

"Are all old timers philosophers?"

"It is not a science. It is the ability to see things clearly and feeling them to the core."

"How can you be lonely in a lovely place like this and surrounded by many others just like you, not to mention so many caretakers?"

Gwen had taken an instant liking to this old and feisty lady. She could not recall the last time she had a really serious and deep conversation with anyone. It was refreshing and exhilarating. A glimpse, perhaps, of the fascination it may have held for Nathan as well. "I would like to visit with you again soon, if you are alright with that?" She patted Florence's sweater-covered arm.

It was a moment before Florence responded. A brief smile revealed yellowing jagged teeth. "I would like that."

Before Gwen left, she asked Maggie if she might talk with the most recent resident. She thought that might prove to be an interesting contrast.

Harvey Feldstain, disabled at age 75 was in a wheelchair in his room. He had been at the Home just shy of three weeks. After introductions Maggie left them alone and Gwen sat in the arm chair.

"So, Harvey, how has it been here so far?"

Harvey did not look quite his age. His frame seemed robust, even if immovable. His hair was still thick and only flecked with grey. His voice was gruff. It was as if he did not want to be bothered by questions. "Comfortable place; nice people; lousy food."

Gwen giggled. "All in one place."

"Not a place I want to be." He took off his glasses and stared at the young woman before him. "I am totally disabled. My spine is messed up. The bones are fused together and there is severe arthritis. Pain comes and goes, mainly in my legs, and nothing has worked so far to help. A shell of my former active self, and forced to be here since I can't do anything for myself. I can't bend over or reach up, and can't even go to the bathroom by myself. I am useless and totally dependent. How am I supposed to feel? My wife has issues and can no longer care for me. The children are spread out all over the country and none is in a position to help. I am not sure they would if they could. I don't want to be a burden to anyone, but here I am Mr. Burden. What more can be said? Sad that a young woman has to see life reduced to a wheelchair and little else."

"We have to learn to deal with the cards we are dealt. Things can come along to lighten a load or give some hope."

"Would be nice although not realistic. My wife has only been able to visit twice so far, and you are my only other visitor. It is not just the physical condition. Mental and emotional limitations can be overpowering. Dealing with immobility and pain is one thing. It is the mind that tortures the soul. When the simplest tasks become impossible a frustration punishes your being. Then, as you wallow in your misery your mind plays tragic games with your past. When you know when you were able you did not do what you should have done, where is the relief? The poor decisions haunt you and obliterate what little good may have been accomplished. For all intents and purposes life is over."

Gwen wondered if she too would be this pessimistic if her future involved being put in a home. "You are very erudite. You have aptly described reality which in one form or another we all have to deal with eventually. I think that the major difference for young people is that they have had less time to make unwise or unnecessary choices. They also probably still believe there is time and opportunity yet to also do something about it. What did you do as a living?"

"I was a college professor for History and Government. Yes, history reveals that even our country has and can make mistakes. Have I told you enough?"

"Yes, thank you. May I visit you again?"

"Sure, if you want to listen to an old man bay at the moon."

Gwen could tell that there was going to be a major problem with the reports. Sure, she could document facts and even embellish them with comments and observations. But, how do you capture and report on the human element? How can she illuminate the life stories? Hearing those stories and thinking about them is one thing. How can one show its impact? How can one help? How could one even try to?

G

At the Clara Bailey Nursing Home, the tour was extensive and Gwen was given all sorts of literature on the place and its history. Since it seemed like a workable approach, she asked if she might interview the longest and shortest residents.

Clyde Hemminger had been a resident for thirteen years. When he had entered the Home, he was diagnosed to have only a year left, but he had made fools of his doctors and defied the odds. At age ninety-eight, he had earned and capitalized on his whispered title of *The Old Philosopher*. He was eager to speak with anyone at anytime, and Gwen could tell right away that the aged fellow had full control of his mental faculties no matter his disheveled physical appearance. There was a worldly wisdom lurking in his response to all of her questions. Yet, for the man himself his own life was a mystery, and he was anxious to explain that to Gwen. "There is a chunk of my past that I do not know actually existed. All of my relatives and acquaintances are gone, and there are no records I could find to deny or validate what might have happened. So, perhaps I am a transport from another world, or does feebleness breed its own story? Does imagination propel a form of reality?"

"Interesting questions," Gwen interjected. "Do you want to tell me the details?"

He grimaced, "I would like to, but it is painful as much as my body absorbs the shoddiness of a long and fruitless life."

"Are these days at the Home any help?"

"I suppose so. My bones get the rest they require. My mind is not always here, so that might be difficult to evaluate."

"Can I do anything for you?" Gwen was earnest in the inquiry.

"No, but any sign of kindness towards an old geezer is appreciated. When it comes from a beautiful woman, there is further contentment."

Gwen was sure she was blushing. "Your eyesight is not good, is it?"

He smiled, thin and chapped lips parting. "Good enough to see what others only pretend to see."

Lydia McCormick had been in the Home for just over a week. The eighty-four year old petite woman was wheelchair bound for many years following a serious automobile accident. Her sister had cared for her, but since that sister's recent passing there had been nobody to take on the responsibility. A cruel fate for so many.

Gwen entered Lydia's room after knocking. The elder woman was propped up in the bed reading a book. "I am Gwen, an employee of the City, and am here to find out how you are doing."

The older woman put down the book, apparently without saving the page she was on and commented in a weak voice, "It is what it is."

"That goes for so many things."

"I prefer not to be here, but we all have to be somewhere while there are still some somewheres."

"You will be well taken care of, I am sure. I will also be checking on you."

"We all need more than care."

"Why do you say that?"

She did not answer right away. "I believe there is a void in everyone. It grows larger as you grow older. What fills it, who knows? It is probably different for different people. But, it is more than the physical."

Gwen related that to the recently discovered void in her own life. "Do you think you may find it here?"

Lydia hesitated. "It can happen anywhere and at any time, I suppose. I think it is too late for me."

"Well, I am going to hope it happens for you here, and soon. You let me know each time I see you, alright?"

"If that is your job."

"It is more than that. I am concerned about you, and I want us to be friends."

"I can't imagine why, but it is not for me to turn you down if that is what you want. I may just thank you along the way."

H

Gwen started her participation in cultural events that evening by going to the concert at the Civic Center. Although weary from the first day on the job, she was excited about going to the event and attained her second wind. The enjoyment not only added to the luster, it confirmed what she had been missing.

Back at the apartment, she mulled over the day's events. She had met an array of interesting folks, people she was drawn to above and beyond the dictates of her employment. Once again she could not escape from the connection to her father's legacy. Her former life had already faded into the background. As she highlighted it all in an email she sent to Casey the following morning, it sank in even further. Her regret was that she had not undertaken this earlier. She wondered if her father had the same kind of regret.

The Wayside House was a very large nursing home and was the oldest in the City. Its facilities had been updated a number of times, but standing before the edifice one could not deny its imposing effect. Gwen had been informed that in the early history of the place there had been patient abuse and a variety of scandals, but in recent years it had garnered a high reputation for beneficial intensive care.

Randolph Waverly was the longest resident at the Home. At age ninety-four he had been there just shy of ten years. His health was poor, in fact Gwen was told he was failing dramatically. Yet, according to the Director, his mind was so sharp that he took delight in relating shocking stories of times and past events just to unsettle anyone who might listen.

That was just the approach he took with Gwen, and after a polite introduction and curt responses to her initial questions, he shouted out to her as she sat besides him, "What do you think about nudism?" He did not give her an opportunity to respond even if she could think of one and then went on to an historical discourse. "In the late 1930's and early 1940's nudism was very popular. It was touted as being healthy, both physically and emotionally. It sort of defied the prudish practice of the rest of society. It was believed to be beneficial for the entire body to be exposed to the sun and fresh air. Whole families were introduced to what is natural and ward off puritanical thoughts as they were exposed to one another. Nudist camps opened up all over the country. My father was a doctor, and he was a firm believer in nudism. I also had two sisters, and each Summer the whole family would spend a week at one of the camps. We would swim, play games and sports, as well as be in the dining area along with other individuals and families. It was wonderful and relaxing. It brought us closer together and reduced petty feelings and thoughts. To me it was part of growing up to see my family members naked as the day they were born. What do you think about that?"

Although Gwen had really never thought about it, she probably would consider herself as a prude. She could not even imagine seeing her mother and father or Albert naked. A few times she had gotten a glimpse of her mother in the shower, and would have the sense that she should not even be looking. With Karl, she always insisted that their love-making be in the dark. "I don't know. I have never thought about it. Possibly, there is some merit to it. If it remained popular, it would no doubt have put a damper on the raging sex industry."

He grimaced. "One of the goddamn rules of this place that only a male employee can bathe a male resident, and a female only a female. Utter nonsense, I say. Especially, old folks. The prudes have taken over and rule the world."

Wilma Morrison, age eighty-two, had been at the home for two months. Gwen found her in an alcove with windows at the back of the Home where residents could sit in the sun in the afternoon. She was a petite woman with thin grey hair, and there was a slight quivering at the corner of her lips. She did not need much coaxing to talk. "I don't belong here," the voice raspy, "Maybe I don't belong anywhere. My life cannot end because it never got started. I married James when I was sixteen. I discovered I could not have children. James was a truck driver, and he was gone for long periods on the road. He had only one dream, and it governed our life. He saved as much money as he could, and we suffered depriving ourselves of many of the good things. His dream was to have a log home in the woods, a place where he could go out the front door and hunt. It became an obsession with him. We bought some land early on, and he quit when he thought there was enough to build the cabin. After it was built, we were in it for only about a month when he was diagnosed with advanced pancreatic cancer and died shortly thereafter. So much for dreams. So much for planning a life that never happened. I could not bear to stay there and sold it. Now, I am here. Nobody cares, and nobody wants me."

Gwen watched a tear roll down Wilma's cheek. A tragic story and a barren life. Gwen braced herself because she sensed there would be many other sad tales of lives wasted or empty. Yet, she was determined to listen to all she could and to encourage the telling of it all. Such might be the best way for her to understand the larger picture and to help when she could. Once again, the shadow of her father was cast over her posture.

I

Each day Gwen would communicate with Casey. There was either a telephone call, a text, or an email. Their distance apart did not detract from their closeness, and each was interested and encouraging about new adventures.

On Saturday morning, Gwen took a walk around the neighborhood to see what her surroundings might be. She wound up on Main Street, the main thoroughfare for quaint shops. It was fun to explore and window shop. She sensed her new found freedom in her moves, her choices.

Gwen came upon an antique shop, *Lost Treasures*, and the window display was filled with interesting items many of which she remembered from her childhood. As if drawn by them, she entered the shop perhaps to find her actual childhood there. The store was not very large, but it was jam packed. Old furniture filled the floor area, and the shelves were cluttered with all sorts of items. She was the only customer. Behind the counter was a tall elderly man with thick silver hair and a beard to match. Wire-rimmed glasses sat on a large nose on an oval face. A Santa Claus image came to mind, although he was not fat and Gwen did not know how jolly he might be. He had a warm smile. "Take your time looking around. This place is filled with special finds, treasures of yesteryear."

Gwen liked his pleasant voice and detected a slight English accent. "I am not a collector and really know little about antiques, but

I have already seen some things that have reminded me of long ago. It makes me want to look back, and I am not sure that is a good thing."

"It is called nostalgia, and it can be comforting to be in touch with a bygone era. Memories are interesting places to linger in. They can be heart-warming or heart-wrenching."

"I have been discovering that for real recently. I have just moved to the City, and this was the first chance I had to explore the neighborhood."

"Well, welcome to the area and I am sure you will find much to see and learn. I hope this shop will be a regular stop for you. There is more than things here. There are stories. There is history."

Gwen leaned against the counter, and with her five foot and three inch height she strained her neck to look into his eyes. She guessed he was about six feet and six inches. "It is a good thing you have high ceilings."

"Comes in handy when I have to hang things up there."

" I bet you played basketball?"

"Yes, when I was a boy in England. I gave it up when the family moved to the States, I wasn't very good at it and, frankly, I found intellectual pursuits more my style."

"Antiques?"

"No, that came much later. I became a teacher, and I taught Civics in high school for many years. Early on, my wife and I became enamored by antiques to help fill up an old large farmhouse we had. When she died, our son was not interested in any of them, so I figured I would try to sell them on my own. I sold the house and moved the antiques to this store and the rest is history. I enjoy the hunt to replace items I sell. I also wanted to live in the City to enjoy concerts and plays, so the decision seemed a natural one. One never can be quite sure where the road takes us."

"I am finding that out myself. How long ago was it that you

started all of this?"

"Coming on twelve years. I am now seventy-three and while I blessedly am in good health I am not sure how much longer I can run the store, especially by myself. I will go on until I run out of steam."

"I have moved in to the City for the same cultural advantages. I left a trite suburban existence and a dumb-founded husband behind. I just started working for the City. I was at the concert last night at the Symphony Hall."

"I was there as well. It was certainly good. I have season tickets for the events there as well as at the Civic Center. It is a small world. I am Leon Hornbecker, by the way, and I am Leo to those close to me."

"Well, pleased to meet you, Leo. I am Gwen Weseley. I am fifty-six and just trying out my new wings."

"Good for you, Gwen. May you fly high and well wherever your flight takes you."

"To be determined."

"Where are you living?"

"I have an apartment at the River House Apartments."

"A small world getting even smaller. I live there as well."

He gave her a tour of the shop, explaining some of the more interesting items. For the next two hours, except when he was helping a customer, they discussed many things. She found him to be interesting and informative, and he explained he read much particularly during slow periods in the store. Gwen told him much about herself, and she was delighted that she could speak such so openly. She even described her relationship with Casey. By the time she left, since he had season tickets to both venues, he invited her to go with him to the events as they unfolded.

Back at the apartment, Gwen stared out the window to the river. It had been a remarkable day for her. She had to admit she was attracted to Leo, despite the age difference. He was easy to talk with, and she felt quite uplifted. She was astute enough to wonder whether her interest in him was romantic or if he merely represented a father figure. Time would tell, as it does with most things.

J

The New Aura Nursing Home was the most recent and innovative nursing home in the City. Located on a quiet street just inside the City line, it had a long waiting list for potential residents. The Director, Janice Longstreet, gave Gwen a detailed tour and she was quite impressed by the variety of programs and projects designed to keep the residents safe and nurtured. At Gwen's suggestion she was taken to meet with the longest and the most recent residents.

Adaline McIver had been a resident for seven years, more than enough time now at age eighty-nine to become a crotchety old shrew. Without a kind word or gesture to anyone, the other residents avoided her and the staff reluctantly assisted her. Gwen was forewarned that an interview might not go well.

Adaline was in the library room, a place she spent most of her day because it was quiet there and few of the other residents showed up. When Janice left the two of them alone, Gwen started the conversation. "Do you like books?"

A moment passed before the frail old woman responded. "They don't talk back."

"I don't talk back either. As a representative of the City, I want to make sure you are being well cared for."

"Why does the City give a damn about me?"

"Because you are a city dweller."

"Even in here?"

"Yes."

"Well then, I am not well taken care of. The place and the people here stink."

"I don't think you really mean that."

"How would you know? You are not here."

"This place has a wonderful reputation, and the folks who run it are very earnest in their duties. You look like you are being taken care of."

"Means nothing."

"Means everything. Tell me about yourself."

She was silent for a moment, and just when Gwen was going to guess there would be no response, the old woman started mumbling. "Not much to tell. I was a librarian, another reason books are my only friends. Loved my work, but couldn't stand people. Still can't. Two husbands died on me, and there is one son living in California and it might just as well be another world. He has nothing to do with me. Life has been hard. I have a right to be bitter."

"I think if you try to have a more positive attitude towards things, you will find out that it is not all bad."

"Not a chance."

Augusta Farrow was the most recent resident and had been there less than a month. At age ninety-two. She had been placed in the home by a daughter who could no longer care for her. A sad story repeated far too often.

Gwen was introduced to Augusta in her room where she was sitting in a wheelchair by the window. She was a frail woman, pronounced wrinkled skin on face and hands. If wrinkles could speak, many a tale of woe would ensue. "Hello, Augusta, I am Gwen and with the City here to make sure you are settling in alright."

There was no response, not even a glance in Gwen's direction. So, Gwen repeated her remarks.

The older woman turned towards her and grinned. "I heard you the first time. I am here and that is all there is to that."

"Why did your daughter have to stop caring for you."

"She lost her job, and her husband is also out of work. She had promised she would never let me go to a home, but here I am. I understand, but I don't understand. It is what it is, and I am the only one who feels bad about it."

"I am sure she feels badly that she had to do this. I feel bad for you as well, although I think you will find in time this may be the most comfortable place to be."

"I suppose."

"Where did you live?"

The voice was getting weaker and Gwen would not linger there. "Not far, and yet very far away. I remember things I never got to finish. Too late for that."

"We all have those thoughts, even younger people."

"Too bad for them as well."

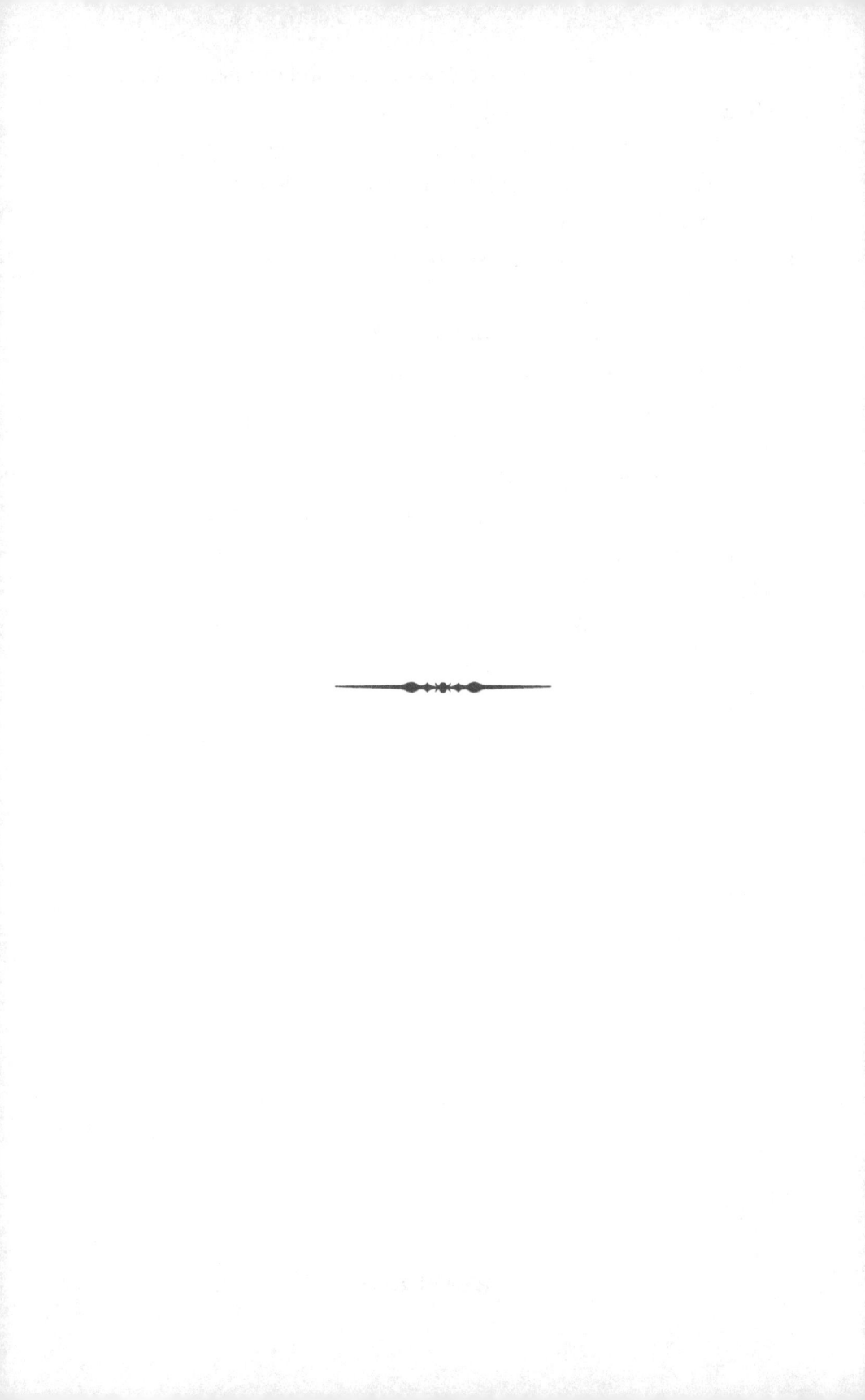

K

On Thursday evening, Gwen and Leo went together to the opening night of a play at the Civic Center. The companionship added to the enjoyment of the program and evening. There was a high comfort level because of the mutual interest and the lack of expectations. They went for dessert afterwards at a bistro close by, and he saw her to the door of her apartment where they planned the next cultural outing .

On Saturday, Gwen made a surprise lunch for him and took it over to the shop. Leo was delighted, and he readily agreed to her offer to help him. She dusted items on the shelves, and he explained the items to her along the way. As they worked side-by-side the conversation was easy and meaningful. Gwen could not fully describe the stirring in her heart, but the feeling was welcome and she basked in it.

Just as she was about to leave the shop, Leo placed his hand on her arm and she felt a jolt in her heart. There was never any such a feeling with Karl. His voice was low and steady, "The shop is closed on Mondays and Tuesdays so I can have some time to myself. One of my hobbies is cooking, and I can only indulge in that on those days. Would you grace me with your presence on Monday after you get home from work and come up to my apartment for dinner?"

The answer came out before she realized it. "I would love to."

"Is there anything you prefer not to eat?"

"Especially if some one else is doing the cooking, I enjoy it all."

"Wonderful. See you then. Thanks again for the lunch and

the help."

On Monday, as she stood before the door to his apartment she thought to herself, "I am really entering a new chapter in my life." She took a deep breath and rang the doorbell.

As expected, Leo's apartment was full of antiques. After they ate the delicious meal he had prepared, he explained many of the artifacts to her. They then sat on the sofa, and she felt relaxed and exhilarated.

"Are you enjoying your new job?", he asked as they sat close together.

"Yes. I am already getting a keen appreciation for older folks and how they look back on their lives."

"I suppose that also includes me. The window looking back is much larger and clearer than the one looking ahead. I don't think any of us can ever say we never wasted the time in our younger years. Perhaps, it is more practical than that. We wasted what we could have done while we were still able to do it."

She patted his arm. "Sounds like you have a story to tell."

"I guess so. To tell a story, the story teller needs to know that someone genuinely wants to listen to it. I can detect that in you, and that is why I think you will be really good at your job."

"I hope so. I have already learned that the listening may be as important as the telling."

"Maybe, more so. There are more tellers than listeners."

"We have known each other for a very short time, but I hope you feel that you can tell me anything. I want to be a good listener."

"I sense that in you. Well, here goes a tale of woe, or rather a tale of deep regret. I have a son who lives in California. He is a screen writer, and does well at that. He has a wife and three children, all strangers to me because I am not close to my son. All of my overtures are rejected. I try to look back and see the wheres and whys, but it is a puzzle. He was closer to my wife, although I cannot remember doing anything to threaten that relationship. There has to be a misunderstanding somewhere along the line, but I am not sure whether it is at my end or his."

"As I have already told you, I have a daughter, Casey, and we have always been close. Yet, recent events I am sure leave her confused and with many doubts. To sidestep having to decide whether she will spend Thanksgiving with me or her father, she has accepted an invitation by her roommate to go home with her for that holiday. Christmas will present a further struggle, I am sure."

"We certainly do not have any control over how others act or react. It is a fine line between being a good influence and bad one."

"Yes, but that does not mean we should not try."

"I don't give up so easily. I think you are the same way."

"I like to think so."

L

Other than the deaths of her mother and father, Gwen had not been close to any other life endings. She figured there would be many more now with her job that she would have to contend with. Yet, she was not fully prepared to confront the news that Randolph Waverly and Florence Ecoatz had died on the same day. There would be no more teases by Randolph when he tried to get to her with his discussion of nudism, and there would be no more serious conversations as she had initially with Florence. Gwen would feel the absence when it happened, and she knew she would reflect on such matters long afterwards. As rewarding as the job promised to be, there would most likely be moments of sadness and despair as lives terminate. She wondered how her father might have dealt with those same feelings in his closing days.

Gwen began systematic visits to the nursing homes. At each visit she would stop in to check on the residents she had already spoken with and then would add some newer folks. There was an insight and appreciation for those in the oldest generation. In the closing days, the winter of their lives, life can be cold and it can be harsh. Even surrounded by others and by events, a form of loneliness can take hold and wear down the will.

In contrast, although Leo was an older person, his capability, both physically and mentally could well rival a younger person. She liked to think he was in the Autumn of his life. A closeness developed with him that she had not known before, and she was frank to admit to herself and to Casey that she was in love for the first time in her life. Leo was warm and affectionate, and Gwen soaked all of that in. They were comfortable with each other, and the sharing of their lives seemed like a natural result. In fact, a genuine dedication to life itself. So, there was no hesitation on her part when he asked that she move in to his apartment with him so that they could share their daily lives. His apartment was larger, and it even had a spare bedroom for Casey to use on her visits.

On one special quiet moment as she watched Leo cooking in the kitchen, she reflected on where she was and where she was going. Propelled by the influence of her father, she had found a satisfying place in her life's journey. It would have been better if it had come earlier, but she welcomed it and knew the contentment and satisfaction would carry her forward.

A person, whether living or dead, can have a major influence on another person. This discovery would be used to positively affect the lives of all who she would make contact with. It was a gift that she would use whenever she could. Her father's ending was her beginning.

www.ingramcontent.com/pod-product-compliance
Lightning Source LLC
Chambersburg PA
CBHW031857170626
46807CB00004B/1775